NEW YORK REVIEW BOOKS
CLASSICS

THE CHILD AND THE RIVER

HENRI BOSCO (1888–1976) was the fifth and only surviving child born to parents of mixed Provençal and Italian descent; his father, whose family was related to Saint John Bosco, made a career as an opera tenor. In 1907, Bosco left his native Avignon to enroll at the University of Grenoble; in 1913 he moved to Algeria to teach French, Latin, and Greek. He fought in World War I, then decamped for Naples in 1920, where he would teach French and write for the next ten years. His first novel, *Pierre Lampédouze*, was published in 1924, and in 1930 he returned to France and married Madeleine Rhodes. They moved to Rabat in 1931, where Bosco again taught classics, served as the president of the Moroccan Alliance Française, and edited the literary journal *Aguedal*. Over the course of his career he published dozens of books of fiction, nonfiction, poetry, and essays, including *Le Mas Théotime* (*The Farm Théotime*, 1945), *L'Enfant et la rivière* (*The Child and the River*, 1945), *Malicroix* (1948, winner of the Prix des Ambassadeurs), and the biography *Saint Jean Bosco* (1959). Bosco was nominated for the Nobel Prize in Literature four times, and was awarded the Grand Prix national des Lettres, the Grand Prix de la Mediterranée, and the Grand Prix de l'Académie française, as well as named a Commander of the Legion of Honor. In 1955, he and Madeleine returned to France, where they divided their time between a farmhouse (La Bastide) in Lourmarin and La Maison Rose in Nice. Bosco is buried in the cemetery in Lourmarin; Madeleine was buried next to him in 1985.

JOYCE ZONANA is the author of the memoir *Dream Homes: From Cairo to Katrina, an Exile's Journey*, and has been published in *The Hudson Review*, *Signs*, and *Meridians*, among other publications. She received a PEN/Heim Translation Fund Grant for her translation of Tobie Nathan's *A Land Like You* and the Global Humanities Translation Prize for her translation of Jóusè d'Arbaud's *The Beast and Other Tales*. Her translation of Bosco's *Malicroix* is published by NYRB Classics.

THE CHILD AND THE RIVER

HENRI BOSCO

Translated from the French by
JOYCE ZONANA

NEW YORK REVIEW BOOKS

New York

THIS IS A NEW YORK REVIEW BOOK
PUBLISHED BY THE NEW YORK REVIEW OF BOOKS
207 East 32nd Street, New York, NY 10016
www.nyrb.com

Originally published in French as *L'Enfant et la rivière.*

This work received support for excellence in publication and translation from Albertine Translation, a program created by Villa Albertine and funded by FACE Foundation.

Library of Congress Cataloging-in-Publication Data
Names: Bosco, Henri, 1888–1976, author. | Zonana, Joyce, translator.
Title: The child and the river / by Henri Bosco; translated by Joyce Zonana.
Other titles: Enfant et la rivière. English
Description: New York: New York Review Books, [2022] | Series: New York
   Review Books classics |
Identifiers: LCCN 2022029487 | ISBN 9781681377421 (paperback) |
   ISBN 9781681377438 (ebook)
Subjects: LCGFT: Novels.
Classification: LCC PQ2603.O627 E5413 2022 |
   DDC 843/.912—dc23/eng/20220628
LC record available at https://lccn.loc.gov/2022029487

ISBN 978-1-68137-742-1
Available as an electronic book; ISBN 978-1-68137-743-8

Printed in the United States of America on acid-free paper.
10 9 8 7 6 5 4 3 2 1

THE CHILD AND THE RIVER

1. TEMPTATION

WHEN I was a child, we lived in the country. The place we called home was no more than a modest tenant farmhouse surrounded by fields. Our life there was uneventful.

My father's aunt, Tante Martine, lived there with us. She was a woman in the old style, always wearing a white piqué cap and pleated gown, with silver scissors dangling from her belt. She lorded it over everyone: dogs, ducks, hens, humans. As for me, I was scolded from morning till night. Never mind that I was docile and well behaved. It made no difference. She scolded. It was because, secretly, she adored me: she scolded to conceal the adoration that, given the slightest opportunity, emanated from her entire being.

All we could see around us were fields, long cypress hedges, small garden plots, and a handful of lonely farmhouses.

This dreary landscape depressed me.

But beyond it flowed a river.

Although everyone talked about it all the time, especially on winter evenings by the fireside, I had never seen it. It played a big role in our family, on account of how it helped or harmed our crops. Sometimes it enriched the soil; at other times it depleted it. It was, apparently, a big, strong, powerful river. In autumn, when the rains came, its waters rose. We could hear them roaring in the distance. Sometimes they rose above the earthen levees and flooded our fields. Later, the waters would recede, leaving mud and silt behind.

In spring, when the alpine snow melted, other waters appeared. The levees gave way under their weight, and again the meadows, as far as the eye could see, were nothing but one vast pond. But in summer, under the burning heat, the river would evaporate. And then little islets of sand and stone would break the current and steam in the sun.

At least, that is what everyone said. I had never seen it for myself.

My father had warned me, "Have fun, go wherever you like. You have plenty of room to roam. But you must never go near the river!"

And my mother had added, "By the river, my child, there are black holes where you can drown; there are snakes in the reeds and Gypsies on the banks."

That is all it took to set me dreaming of the river night and day. When I thought about it, a chill crept down my spine, but I had a burning desire to know it.

Every now and then, an old poacher would stop by our house. He was a tall man, rough, with a face like a knife blade and a keen, cunning eye. Everything about him—the knotty arms, the calloused foot, the nimble fingers—suggested strength and skill. He would show up like a shadow, soundlessly.

"Look, it is Bargabot," my father would say. "He is bringing us some fish."

Indeed.

Bargabot would set a basket of shimmering fish on the

kitchen table. They amazed me. Silver bellies shone through the algae; bluish backs and spiny fins.

They were water creatures, fresh from the river.

"Bargabot, how do you manage to catch such fine ones?" my father would ask.

"Mr. Boucarut, the Good Lord takes pity on the poor," Bargabot would answer evasively. "And besides, I have the knack."

We could never get anything more out of him.

One day when I was alone in the house, Bargabot showed up out of the blue, as usual. He was carrying a huge shad at the end of a hook.

"Look," he said, "it is yours, I am giving it to you."

He laid the fish along the edge of the table. Then he gave me an odd look. "Little one, little one," he murmured, "you have a good little mug, a fisherman's mug. Have you never caught a fish?"

"No, Mr. Bargabot, I am not allowed to go by the river."

He shrugged. "What a pity! But if I had you with me, I would show you some good spots where no one ever goes, especially on the islands…"

Once he had told me that, I could not sleep.

Often, at night, I would think about those marvelous spots, hidden in the middle of the woods or on the banks of islands, where no one but Bargabot ever went.

Sometimes, Bargabot would show me lovely blue-steel fishhooks or finely carved cork bobbers.

Bargabot was my hero: I idolized him. And yet his keen gray eyes filled me with fear. And out of fear, I kept my fondness for him hidden.

When he was around I was a bit scared; when he was

gone, I missed him. Whenever I heard his rope-soled shoes slipping through the yard, my heart would start to pound. He soon saw how I felt about him. But he pretended not to care, which tortured me. Sometimes, for a couple of weeks, we would see nothing of him. I could not sit still. A wild longing would make me want to run to the river. But I was afraid of my father. He did not fool around.

Winter, the same old story. It is cold out, the wind howls, the snow falls; it would be madness to roam the countryside. It feels good in front of the fire, and so there you stay. But in springtime the wind is gentle, the weather mild. People need air and movement. This need would take hold of me as it takes hold of everyone. And I had such an intense longing to escape I shook with fear.

I was always on the verge of giving in, one fine day, and heading out for adventure. All I needed was the chance.

The chance came. Here is how.

My parents had to leave for a few days. While they were gone, Tante Martine, naturally, took charge of the house. As I have already said, Tante Martine was a tyrant. But once she was alone with me, I had all the freedom I could want. She longed to be free herself, and how could she be free if she watched over me from morning till night? Whoever tyrannizes others tyrannizes himself. Tante Martine knew this. Which is why she gave me free rein—so she could come and go as she pleased.

And she came and went. From the top to the bottom of the house, she came and went. She came and went by day, she came and went by night; she came and went at dawn, she came and went at dusk. Always barely perceptible, as if on little mouse feet. When my parents were home, she stayed more or less in one place; but they were hardly out the door before she started to come and go. I never saw her anymore, but I heard her rummaging around from room to room. Now she burrowed into the darkness of the cellar; now she slipped into the pantry.

What was she doing? God knows! I heard mysterious sounds: a plank creaked; a crate tumbled with a bang...Then silence...But of all the spots our old house harbored, Tante Martine's favorite was the attic. She went up every afternoon and often stayed until first dark. It was her favorite refuge, her paradise. Up there were ancient, goatskin-covered trunks, studded with brass nails and crammed with time-worn clothes—flowered jackets, satin vests, yellowed lace, embroidery, silver-buckled pumps, polished boots. And what dresses! All pink silks, lamé trim, gold sequins, puce ribbons, red, purple. Faded, musty colors, yes, but so delightful! Because everything still smelled of lavender and russet apples. I was wild about all of it. And these were not the only wonders. Stately family portraits hung from nails. In one corner, painted dishes were stacked up. Two silver chandeliers lay on an ebony case. Leather-bound books were scattered on the floor amid a pile of yellowed papers, a rat's nest... And from the ceiling, an old straw-stuffed crocodile was suspended by its tail and head, a gift from Uncle Hannibal, a sailor.

When Tante Martine climbed up to the attic, nothing in the world could have dragged her out. She would double-lock herself in, and I was not permitted to follow her.

"Go play in the garden," she would tell me, "I need to put the old clothes in order."

I took the hint. Alone, with nothing to do, I would wander through the house for a while and then sit under the fig tree by the well.

That is where, one fine April morning, temptation caught me unawares. It knew how to speak to me. It was a springtime temptation, one of the sweetest there is, I think, for anyone who is open to clear skies, tender leaves, and newly blossomed flowers.

That is why I succumbed.

I headed out across the fields. Oh, how my heart was pounding! Spring shone in all its glory. And when I opened the meadow gate, a thousand scents of plants, trees, and fresh bark leapt up to greet me. Without looking back, I raced toward a thicket where bees were dancing. The air, laden with pollen, throbbed with their wingbeats. Farther off, an almond orchard—where the new year's first wood pigeons were cooing—looked like a drift of snowy blossoms. I was intoxicated.

The narrow paths slyly beckoned me. "Come! What difference can a few more steps make? The first turn is not far. You will stop when you get to the hawthorn." These pleas made me lose my head. Once on those paths that snaked between hedges brimming with birds and blueberries, how could I stop?

The farther I went, the more the path's power took possession of me. The longer I walked, the wilder it grew.

The garden plots disappeared, the soil became richer, and here and there tall gray grasses or dwarf willows waved. The gusty wind smelled of damp silt.

All of a sudden, right in front of me, a levee rose. It was a high earthen bank, topped by poplars. I clambered up and saw the river.

It was wide, flowing West. Swollen by snowmelt, its powerful waters coursed along, with a cargo of trees. The waters were heavy and gray, and occasionally large whirlpools formed for no reason, engulfing the debris that had been uprooted upstream. Whenever they met an obstacle, the waters roared. They charged the bank in one huge torrent, some five hundred yards wide. Midstream, a wilder current swept past, marked by a dark crest that sliced through the silty waters. It looked so terrifying I shuddered.

Downstream, an island rose, parting the current. Steep banks thickly overgrown with willows made the approach difficult. It was a huge island, dense with poplar and birch. Tree trunks ferried down by the river were crashing onto its tip.

When I turned back to the bank I saw that, right at my feet, beneath the levee, a small cove sheltered a beach of fine sand. The waters were calm there. It was a dead spot. I went down to it. Wild privet, giant osiers, and dark alders formed a roof over my head.

In the half dark, thousands of insects were buzzing.

On the sand, I could see traces of bare feet. The footprints went from the water to the levee. They were big, strong, like an animal's. I grew frightened. The place was lonely, wild. I could hear the waters roaring. Who haunted this hidden cove, this secret beach?

Across from me, the island remained silent. Yet I thought it looked menacing. I felt alone, weak, exposed. But I could not leave. A mysterious force kept me bound to this lonely place. I searched for a bush where I could hide. Was someone spying on me? I slipped under a thorny shrub for shelter. The soft ground was covered in supple, springy moss. Invisible, I waited there, studying the island.

At first I saw nothing. The shade from the leaves stretched

over me; the insects danced on; every now and then a bird flew off; the water flowed, slowed by the curve of the beach. Time passed, unchanging, and the air grew warmer. I dozed off.

I must have slept for a long time.

What woke me? I do not know. When I opened my eyes, stunned to find myself under the bush, the sun was low and the afternoon was drawing to a close. Nothing seemed to have changed around me. And yet I stayed still, deep within my hideout, waiting for something to happen.

All of a sudden, in the middle of the island, from among the leafy trees, a wisp of clear blue smoke rose up.

The island was inhabited. My heart pounded. I carefully studied the opposite shore, but to no avail. No one appeared. After a while, the smoke faded; bit by bit, it seemed to sink back into the clustered trees, as if absorbed by the invisible earth. No trace of it remained.

Night was falling. I emerged from my retreat and returned to the beach.

What I found terrified me. Right beside the first tracks I had seen on the sand, others, still fresh, marked the ground. So, while I had been sleeping, someone had passed right by my refuge. Had they seen me?

Night was now arriving behind the reeds. A bird abruptly fluttered up from the rushes. It cried out, and from the island a mournful moan replied.

I fled.

I did not reach the house until it was pitch black out.

I will let you guess how Tante Martine greeted me.

"Vagabond! Drifter! Good-for-nothing!"

She sniffed me. "You smell like mud. And just look at your hair!"

It was a tangle of leaves and thorns.

"Go comb it!"

I did as I was told, sheepish, silent. I knew Tante Martine. Anger, yells. But it never went any further.

"Are you not ashamed?"

Of course I was ashamed, but when you are ashamed you keep your mouth shut, and so I did.

"What if I told your father, huh, Pascalet"—Pascalet is my name—"you know all too well what he would do, do you not?"

I knew perfectly well, but I also knew Tante Martine. Everything in her was saying, "Rascal! You are lucky Tante Martine has a weakness for the little scoundrel Pascalet. After all, way back when, your father was just the same!"

Beneath her menacing look, Tante Martine was relenting. "And you must be hungry, no?"

I was hungry and I admitted it.

"Well of course you are," she grumbled as she heated the skillet. "Since seven in the morning! Poor boy! I bet your head is spinning."

I lied. "Yes, Tante Martine, my head is spinning sure enough, but not too fast."

"All I have is a little soup to give you . . . and two toma-toes . . . and some sausage."

We heard a footstep. Bargabot entered the kitchen.

He had never looked so tall to me. He wore his wild look. Tante Martine was so startled she almost dropped the skillet. But Bargabot paid her no mind.

"Here, I have brought some carp. Cook them. You will not refuse me a glass of wine," he said.

And he sat down at the table.

Tante Martine took the basket of fish.

We could hear her scraping the scales. The oil was smoking in the skillet. We invited Bargabot to join us. Tante Martine brought out the jug of wine, brown bread, vinegar.

Bargabot drew a long knife from his pocket. He cut himself a generous chunk of bread, placed two fish on it, and traced a cross over the food with his blade. Then he dug in.

We watched him. He did not say a word. His body smelled like the river.

We were not thinking about eating. He could tell. Our eyes met.

"You need to eat, my boy," he murmured. "I caught this fish for you. It is from the river. You know the river quite well, do you not?—with its islands and its thickets, where it is easy to hide?"

I turned white. Tante Martine was eyeing me. But Bargabot picked up the finest fish on the tray and set it on my plate. With surprising delicacy, he slit it, removed the bones, and poured a few drops of oil and a dash of vinegar on the flesh. "Here you are," he said, "help yourself."

Tante Martine pouted a little. We ate the meal in silence.

When the plates had been removed, Bargabot, still silent, began to trace strange shapes on the table with the tip of his long knife: bizarre fish, some bristling with spikes, some all head, huge, with gaping, greedy mouths. There were also fantastic snakes and water turtles.

Tante Martine and I were silent, fascinated by these odd creatures. Suddenly Bargabot muttered, "Smells like a storm."

Soon after, we heard thunder in the distance.

Bargabot rose and said, "Good night, I have no time to lose."

And he promptly disappeared.

All night long it thundered. The thunder really roared, without letup. Rolling darkly, it blanketed the whole countryside. The lightning opened and closed like scissors of fire. From deep down, the ground echoed the roar. Huddled under my covers, I was thinking about the river. How eerily it must be gleaming under the lightning's blue flame.

Wind-driven, slanting rain lashed the house, which groaned from top to bottom under the fury of the downpour. The storm lasted until morning. Then, grumbling, it withdrew. The sun pierced a cloud and the fields gleamed in its glow.

It took three full days of heat to dry up the soil.

During those three days, I did not stir.

Tante Martine resumed her coming and going. Caught up in her passion, she had forgotten my escapade.

2. THE ISLAND

I SET OUT again one Tuesday morning. Day was just dawning. Tante Martine was still asleep in her room. She had been up poking around until midnight. I took advantage of her slumber and stuffed a small sack with supplies: figs, nuts, and a big chunk of bread. An hour later, I was on the riverbank.

What glory! The stream was now limpid, and the bright blue, rain-washed sky, where the laughing wind was driving two little clouds, lay reflected in the clear water that flowed toward the hilly horizon. The terrible, black-crested current at the center no longer broke up this smooth mirror. The river was smiling between its banks, tinted pink by the dawning day. A kingfisher flitted up the length of the island, and a morning breeze rustled through the reeds.

I went back up the bank toward a shack. On four stilts, it overhung the water. A footbridge offered access.

Inside, on a hammock, was a pallet of dry algae. An old net hung from the ceiling. In a corner were some cooking utensils.

"This must be where Bargabot sleeps when he fishes and hunts," I thought.

Below the shack, I could see a small beach. A rowboat was tied to one of the stilts.

It was old, worm-eaten. Water seeped through the badly

joined planks. No paint on the hull. Sun and wind had long since flaked it off. The oars were gone. A frayed hemp rope held the boat to the stilt. The water was so calm the slack line drooped in the river.

This calm, this quiet, soon tempted me. I climbed down to the boat and, after a moment's hesitation, set my foot on the gunnel. It sagged under my weight. This sagging worried me. But the boat righted itself. I sat down carefully on the center bench and did not move. The boat, the water, and the bank all seemed stationary, and despite the mute terror gripping my chest, I was happy.

Because, with my back to the bank, I saw nothing before me except the river. It was gliding by. Farther away downstream, the island, caught in the sun's first rays, was beginning to emerge from the morning mists. Poplars, elms, and birches formed a tangled heap from which, little by little, big swatches of leaves were coming clear in the light. At the tip, a big blue boulder jutted out of the water, roughly breaking it. The water seethed angrily. But so pink was the bank of the island, and such was the fragrance of trees, plants, and wildflowers that came wafting on the gentle breeze, that I was wonderstruck. Again, as on the other evening, smoke rose from the wood.

"It is Bargabot building a fire," I thought. "He must have fished last night." Why was I not on the island? I was dreaming of it . . .

The boat was still. Not one visible current reached the shelter of my little haven. I contemplated the silent, gliding waters, whose movement enchanted me . . .

I lost all sense of time, place, and even of self—I could no longer tell what was moving, my boat or the river. Was the river fleeing, or was I the one who, miraculously, without oars, was heading upstream? God only knows how I had left shore; yet here I was, already seeing the shack's four stilts moving away. They were moving away...were they moving away?

Abruptly, I came back to myself. Where was I? Between the boat and the shack, the rope lay loose in the water. Caught in an invisible current, I was drifting. I tried to catch a branch as it passed, but it eluded me. I was moving smoothly, steadily, farther away from the shore. I was frozen with fear. Because the water, calm at first, was pulling me out into the mainstream, and I could see the huge sweep of the river rapidly coming at me.

It was all in motion, and its deep immensity was driving me toward the looming boulder at the tip of the island where the waves crashed and seethed.

The waters grew more violent. Faster and faster, they swept the old boat. It creaked. Water rose through the cracks. Massive whirlpools struck me crosswise, spinning the boat around. Whenever one side of it met the shock of the water, it tilted dangerously. I was heading straight for the boulder. It was coming at me, terrifying. I closed my eyes. The water roared, and the boat, caught in an eddy, spun slowly around. The hull jolted as it scraped against something. We came to rest on a bed of gravel. I opened my eyes. I was saved. The boat had come to a halt on a gently sloping beach at the tip of the island. In the distance, the churning went on around the boulder that I had missed.

In one leap, I was on land.

That is when I started to sob.

It was only after I had cried my eyes out that I realized my predicament. Two hundred yards of deep water separated me from my shore, the shore where people live, where smoke rises from safe, warm homes. A mile away, on this blue morning, under a stand of pine and plane trees, mine must be sending its plume of smoke into the sky. It was nine o'clock. Tante Martine had already lit her wood fire. She was searching for me. I felt a pang of despair. How could I leave the island? Whom could I call on for help?

I sat on a root and tried to think. Alas! My thoughts led nowhere. They all said, "Pascalet, you are lost." But that hardly mattered. One question alone tormented me: "What will Tante Martine think? It is still only nine o'clock, and already she is suffering. What will she feel at midnight? Because at midnight you will still be here, my dear Pascalet. And the water will be as black as ink by then, gliding darkly by."

Gloomy, gloomy thoughts...

That is when the light breeze brought me the acrid smell of burnt wood. The memory of the hearth, whose smoke I had seen twice through the trees, came back to me. "I must see it," I told myself. And I threaded my way under the bushes. I arrived at the edge of a clearing.

At the center of this clearing stood a hut. Broad and round, it rose up like a sugarloaf. A sack was hanging in front of the door.

Three stones had been set on the beaten earth. That is where a small fire was burning. The smoke from it licked a large, black cauldron—a strange sort of creature with two little ears and a big belly.

A young girl squatted in front of the fire, stirring the coals with a stick. A black cat dozed in front of the hut. A few hens were pecking.

Who were these people, so poor they had to live in this crude branch hut?

The little girl was dressed in rags. Dark eyes, sooty skin. What a strange creature!

She had big copper hoops in her ears. Now and then she hummed softly. A donkey casually wandered through the clearing. Beyond the hut, under a tree, I caught a vague glimpse of a large brown mound. This mound worried me. I could not identify it because it was too far off. It remained unmoving. Was it an animal?

Swirls of steam escaped from the cauldron. It smelled good. A crow came from the woods and perched on the girl's bare shoulder. She spoke to it. Astonished, I got up to see her better. The girl turned her head and looked my way. But she remained impassive. Had she seen me?

An old woman emerged from the hut. She was lean and fierce looking. She grabbed a rooster by the neck and yelped wildly as she slit its throat over the fire.

The brown mound rose, groaned, got down on all fours, and the bear—it was a bear!—lumbered toward the fire. When it neared the cauldron, it sniffed the air, its muzzle pointed my way. I fled.

I ran without stopping to the tip of the island, where I searched for a good hiding place. I had barely settled down when I heard lapping water. Anxiously, I looked out. A boat was coming from the shore toward the island. Four men were aboard. Four big louts, harsh and rough, rougher than Bargabot. Gypsies! This time I was done for, truly done for!

They landed, then hid their boat behind a rise. They dragged out a child—a boy my age. He had been tied up. One of the men lifted him onto his shoulders. I could clearly see the boy's face. It was dark like those of his captors, and just as wild. But nothing in it betrayed fear. With his eyes closed and his lips clamped shut, he seemed made of stone. He was borne off. The four men vanished beneath the trees.

I was alone.

It was noon. I was hungry. But I did not dare touch my supplies. The slightest movement seemed risky: an awkward gesture, a broken branch—anything could betray me. I would be discovered, captured, tied up!

All afternoon, I did not dare leave my shelter, a small hollow carved into the rock and concealed by two cranberry bushes. I was waiting for a miracle: someone would show up on shore, a fisherman perhaps...

But no one showed up. Evening came.

I was surprised, because I had never really seen evening before. At least not the way I was seeing it now, all dark and blue in the East, with great branching trees of stars. Its immensity stupefied me.

As daylight dimmed, the sky, deepened by shadow, sank from one abyss to another and great celestial shapes mysteriously appeared. These were constellations unfamiliar to me. Later, I learned their names: the Great Bear, Betelgeuse, Orion, Aldebaran. At the time, not knowing them, I was happy just to admire their nighttime sparkle. They were burning silently, very far away. Their fires shone trembling in the dark gleaming river. Night had fallen, and the fast-moving waters pushed up so powerfully against the island that I was afraid. Huddled in my hideout, I closed my eyes and tried to ignore them. The confused murmur of the river reached me even so, troubling my soul. I felt small, frail, reduced to this little bit of myself, shivering in a beast's lair.

I could have touched the cold water with my foot. Huge drifts rapidly slid by below my hideout. It was a treacherous, terrifying spot that soon filled me with dread. After a while, I could no longer stand it. I crawled out and scaled the bank. What would I not have given to hear a human voice, to see a human face! But who could I call to my rescue? The people on this island stole children, no doubt about it. What cruelty! But still they were human. They had a hut, a poor thing, yes, but one that sheltered their human sleep. And they had a fire. Not far from my hideout, in red bursts, its flames lit up the foliage. A hearth was burning there, a true hearth, with embers and warm ash, an iron cauldron, food, comforting light . . .

The more I thought about that hearth, the more I was tempted to slip over to the hut, if only to see, on this night when I felt so alone, human fire. And so furtively I threaded my way through the undergrowth. Moving like a cat, without snapping a twig, I managed by some miracle to make it to the clearing, where, crouched under a prickly holly, I watched.

The old witch squatted in front of the fire. The girl poked at it.

The woman, ladle in hand, was slowly stirring some sort of infernal brew in the cauldron. The dog, on his rump, sat staring at her and sniffing the steam. His ears were pointy. The bear roamed freely around the clearing. Because I was downwind from the camp, the animals could not pick up my scent.

Seated on the ground not far from the fire, three men were eating.

A fourth stood holding a whip.

They had tied the child's arms and legs to a post.

The man had just finished whipping him. The whip's lash had scarred the boy's back, naked to the waist. When the flame rose, I could see three long dark stripes of blood on the bronze flesh.

The man was speaking harshly to the child. I did not understand his words. He spoke a strange language.

The child, far from trembling, answered so angrily that his tormentor flogged him again.

The whistling strap slashed his skin. The child fell silent.

He was a handsome child, sturdy, taller than me and stronger, most likely a young Gypsy.

Under the lash, he bit his lips and his eyes closed in pain, but he did not whimper.

As if unwillingly, the man left the child and went to eat. Then he and his three companions moved away from the fire and went into the hut to sleep. The old woman rose and went in as well. Only the dog, the bear, and the girl were left in the clearing. The child tied to the post had not opened his eyes again.

The bear came close, sniffed him. The child did not stir. The bear lay down almost at his feet and did not move again. The dog ran into the woods to hunt.

The girl stretched out in front of the fire and was soon asleep.

The boy raised his head and opened his eyes. Slowly, he looked all around the clearing. His gaze came toward me, and when it passed in front of me, I shivered. And yet he could not have seen me. I was buried under branches and leaves; still, his gaze reached me, and I was touched. I was seized by a wild idea. "Oh," I thought, "I should crawl to the post and undo the cords." I did not have the courage. The camp, barely asleep, was right there, with its sorceress, its bear, its four cruel men, and that girl, all of whom could be suddenly awakened by the smallest noise.

How did I manage to forget all that? I emerged from my bush and stepped into the clearing.

And so the child saw me. The fire lit me fully. He saw me but did not react. His eyes shone, his wolf's teeth gleamed between his drawn lips, and, without betraying the least emotion, he watched me come toward him like a phantom.

When I reached the post, I took hold of the cord and tried to untie it. But the knots were too tight, impossible to undo.

"There is a knife by the cauldron," the child whispered. "My name is Gatzo."

But the girl was sleeping by the cauldron.

"She will wake up," I replied, already trembling.

"Oh, are you frightened?" the captive murmured.

And he bowed his head. His pain upset me. I left him and went toward the fire. I walked lightly, as if in a dream.

The knife was on the ground, but the girl had somehow tightened her grip around it in her sleep.

I took her hand, gently spread the fingers, and slid the knife out.

"Oh!" the girl sighed, "I must be dreaming…"

She brought her hand to her face and, frightened by whatever she saw, rolled away from me. Sleep took her again.

I returned to the post.

The cords that bound the boy's arms were soon cut. A night bird moaned. The bear woke up.

Surprised to see me, he reared, grunted, and thrust his huge muzzle at me.

"Do not be afraid," the child reassured me. "I know how to talk to him."

"Agalaoû, Agalaoû, Rekschah! Arazadoulce!" he said.

His voice, as it shaped those sounds, shifted from gruff to gentle. The bear relaxed. It curled up again, sighed resignedly, and fell back asleep.

I cut through the last of the bonds.

We stole away from the camp.

No moon. It was so dark that, without my companion, I would have been lost a thousand times over. He made his way through the shadows with eyes that shone like a cat's, and he was holding my hand.

"Where are we going?" I asked.

"To the boat," he breathed.

We reached it soon enough.

"It is our lifeline," he told me.

I confessed my fear. "We are definitely going to drown, the current is too strong."

"They will kill us if we stay," he replied abruptly. "Do not be afraid. I know the river."

We struggled to drag the boat out from under the bush where the Gypsies had hidden it.

Gatzo waded into the water and pushed while I boarded the boat. I was struck by his strength. As soon as the current caught us, he clambered aboard.

"Stay up front," he ordered. "I will steer."

He set an oar over the stern and steered. An eddy slowly swept us away from the island, which looked huge and dark to me, with its towering trees amid those great, moving waters.

We skirted the island for a while. Then we caught the current slantwise and steered toward midstream.

"Where are we off to?" I asked timidly.

Gatzo did not answer. I could barely see him. But from his breathing and his groans, I could tell he was leaning into the oar with all his might. The river was strong and did not let you navigate without great effort.

3. STILL WATERS

WE TRAVELED the better part of the night. I stayed up. At first, Gatzo hewed to the center of the river. He seemed to know it. A swift, strong current bore us along. Later, I could see the trees on shore drawing closer. They were coming at us confusedly, and we slowed down, making our way into a channel between two dark walls of vegetation. Soon, the channel grew so narrow that we brushed damp leaves as we advanced. Then the channel widened, and on a flat stretch of water that looked vast in the faint starlight, the boat, moving more and more slowly, came to a halt.

We moored. Gatzo turned to me and asked me my name. "Pascalet."

"Well then, Pascalet. You are safe now. Do as I do. Sleep. Good night!"

And he stretched out on the bottom of the boat.

I followed his lead. I was tired, and although the planks were hard, soon I fell asleep. That night I slept well.

Now, all this took place a long, long time ago, and today I am very nearly an old man. But for the rest of my life, however long I may live, I will never forget those early days when I lived on the water. Those beautiful days are still with me in all their freshness. What I saw then I still see today, and when

I think about it now, I become again the child enchanted by the beauty of the watery world he discovered upon awakening.

When I opened my eyes, day was dawning. At first I saw the sky. Just the sky. It was gray and violet, with just a little pink high up on a thread of cloud. Still higher, the wind was weaving other threads through a light lattice of mists. In the East, a pale gold fog was slowly rising above the river. A bird called out; it might have been a warbler. Its sharp, restive cry awakened a frog's discreet croaks. Then a flight of wet wings ruffled the tufts of reeds, and all around our boat the confused murmur of as yet unseen water creatures arose. All the sounds —sighs, furtive movements, a ripple, droplets; a frightened rat's dive; a lively bird's clattering splash; a teal slipping through the bulrushes; the reed warbler's hoarse call; an oriole's sudden whistle; and, now, beneath a willow on shore, a turtledove's cooing. I was listening. Every so often, the dawn breeze drifted across this unreal world, these spaces made solely of sound, and the aquatic plants, awakening from silence, bent by the wind, rustled gently. The boat did not move. Like a cork bobber, it seemed so light it barely rested on the water.

On the floor of the boat, my companion was asleep. He was lying with his head thrown back. Sleep had immobilized his face. It was a dark, muscular face, with high cheekbones. A short nose, its two small nostrils puffed out. The lips looked as if they were fiercely clenched over his sleep, and two large black lids weighed heavily on his closed eyes. In this way, sleep's mask perfectly molded his wild little soul. Nothing stood between that soul and the flesh of the face.

But life was briskly rising up into it.

When the sun, passing over the reeds, reached the face, its eyes suddenly opened.

Gatzo saw me and smiled. On that severe face the hard

features suddenly softened to form a very tender smile that moved me deeply.

"Pascalet," Gatzo murmured.

And I smiled back at him. We were friends.

That is how the time of still waters began. For ten days, we lived secretly on one of the river's backwaters.

"We will be safe here for a while," Gatzo assured me. "Later, we will see."

This backwater was hidden deep in the lowlands, on the left bank across from my native shore. We were separated from land by impenetrable stands of aquatic plants. They concealed us.

Along the bank, a thick wall of alders. Closer to us, guelder rose, gorse, and, in heavy clumps, walls of reeds. All the reeds: bulrushes, sword grass, cattails, sweet flag. Hardy and strong, they rose up from the virgin silt, forming dense islands here and there amid the dark waters.

The backwater dwindled into countless channels. Some meandered through the archipelago of plant life only to disappear, little by little, under a green vault. Others burrowed beneath the willows. They were all mysterious. Their waters slept. Yet from time to time an unseen current bore along an arrowhead blossom or a marsh trefoil.

These visions enchanted me. Gatzo, for his part, seemed indifferent. He spoke little. At first his brusque ways surprised me, but soon I got used to them. His rescue, our flight—he never mentioned them. His friendship was unspoken. We got along, because I too like silence. But for reasons different from his. He was silent so he could plan our next moves. All his thoughts were about our needs—fishing, finding a good mooring, stretching a canvas screen to block the sun, securing shelter, cooking a meal. When he did say a few words, it was never just for the sake of talking. He never made a useless gesture. Each word had a purpose, each gesture a goal. He was sparing with his soul. But his soul was there. I felt it beside me, enclosed in his dark body, perhaps a bit somber. It was inseparable from his violent life and was fed on bitter blood. I suspected it to be both vengeful and loyal.

Everything in me, except the taste for silence, contrasted with Gatzo's nature. When I am silent, it is for the pleasure of being silent. This pleasure does not rule out a few thoughts; still, they are only idle thoughts—thoughts that stroll, wander, roam, or else pass into the half sleep that leads to vain dreams. I do not actively think then, but I casually follow the reflections of the vague images that fill me, and if I stay silent, it is because silence gives these fleeting shadows better access to a soul enchanted by their appearance.

"You are asleep on your feet," Gatzo would say, annoyed.

He himself separated sleeping from waking with cruel clarity.

"When I sleep," he would say, "I do it right. I close my eyes and do not think about anything. It relaxes me. When you sleep, you toss and turn, you speak, you ruin your sleep..."

I said nothing in reply; he was right. But I was hurt.

The first day on the backwater was beautiful. I had never known anything like it. It remains the most beautiful day of my life. First, we explored the boat, which harbored treasures. Two full chests. One, in front, contained fishing gear—

horsehair, bobbers, hooks, lines, baskets, traps, lures. The other, in back, was crammed with supplies stored in iron boxes to protect them from the damp.

"They often used to travel far from the island," Gatzo said, "without being able to restock. That is why..."

I would have liked to have heard much more, but Gatzo limited his disclosure to this.

The discovery of these supplies thrilled us. Here was coffee, sugar, a barrel of flour, dried beans, spices, a flask of oil, and the like. In short, enough to live on for more than a week.

As for the boat, it was fitted with four oars.

The hull seemed completely watertight. The paint was not peeling. On the back of the chest in the bow was an inlaid copper compass rose. It filled us with wonder. It had thirty-two points and bore the names of sixteen winds, each more beautiful than the last: Labé, Gregali, Tramontane...

"We should polish it," Gatzo briskly declared. "It is our good luck charm."

We dropped everything to polish it. It sparkled.

All around the rose, in big gold letters, we saw the boat's name, *La Marouette*, the Little Crake.

"They stole it," Gatzo said. "I know where. But it is far from here."

He pointed upstream.

I could barely see faint hills turning blue.

"There?" I asked.

"There," Gatzo replied.

Where was it? And from where had Gatzo come to the island? Who was he?

I wondered without daring to question this boy who never asked me anything. Because I too was a mystery to Gatzo. My presence on the island, my sudden arrival, should have intrigued him. Yet he did not show the slightest curiosity about these miracles that I, for my part, found astonishing.

Because there were moments when I told myself I was dreaming—a delicious, terrifying dream.

Could it really be, after so many adventures, that I was here on this boat with a child whose name was the only thing I knew? On this hidden boat, lost among the reeds, on the river's backwater?

And could I be here with so much delight, and no remorse? Because I felt no remorse, even when I thought of Tante Martine. She must be sighing, sobbing, screaming, pulling out her hair, the poor thing!

I saw her, I heard her, I felt a little sorry for her, but without much conviction, because to be here—floating on these four light planks on a sunny, breezy morning—filled me with living happiness, true happiness. It was on my skin, in my flesh, in my blood; it went all the way down to my soul. I did not know what a soul was. At that age you do not. But I clearly sensed that this joy was more than my body, and I said to myself, "Pascalet, it is the angel of the Lord stirring with pleasure within you. Treat it well."

I treated it well, but casually enough.

Because we worked hard that day.

First, we changed our mooring.

"Here, right in the middle of the water, if anyone comes by, they will see us," Gatzo wisely observed. "Let us move."

With little oar strokes, we approached the reeds.

We moored by three thickly overgrown islets. One of them rose slightly above the water. The dried silt ground was solid enough.

Tall grasses grew there, a few shrubs, and, on the edge, some lovely marsh pennywort.

"We will build our fire here," Gatzo declared. "There is some deadwood. Let us dig an oven."

We dug it. Gatzo found two large, flat river stones. We piled up some deadwood and twigs.

"And now we will fish for our dinner," Gatzo decreed.

He put hooks on two lines. I was new to the art of fishing. He taught me.

Squatting, he took his post at one end of the boat.

"Watch me and keep still," he warned.

The two lines drifted lazily, and the cork floated, motionless, on the dark, limpid water.

Nothing moved. Not a breeze in the reeds. Not a current in the water. Only an aimless butterfly fluttering, pink and gold, two inches above the clear, still water. Sometimes it skimmed the water. Did it drink? . . . All around our refuge, shadows cast by reeds and willows filtered the sun's rays; only a half light hovered over the mysterious wet expanse. Perhaps, beneath these dull gleams, the water's invisible empire was uninhabited. I was inclined to believe it, and yet, every now and then, in the underwater half dark, we thought we glimpsed a flash of silver glide by. It promptly vanished. And then a few air bubbles, released from some algae, drifted up.

Gatzo caught four smelt and a loach.

I caught a minnow.

From then on, our life was thrilling. We had food on hand—and what food! Because this was not ordinary food—bought, prepared, and served by others—but our own food, food we had fished ourselves, and which we had to clean, season, and cook ourselves.

Now, the secret gifts of this food grant miraculous powers to anyone who partakes of it. Because its life is joined with nature's. Which is why, immediately, a wondrous link was forged between us and the elements. Water, earth, fire, and air were revealed to us.

Water, which had become our true ground: we were dwelling on water, drawing life from it.

Earth, more or less unseen, holding the water in its strong arms.

Air, from which come winds, birds, insects.

Air, where clouds move so lightly. Air, calm and stormy. Air, where light and shadow spread. Air, where omens take shape.

Lastly, fire, without which food is uncivilized. Fire, which warms and comforts. Fire, which creates a camp. Because without fire, a resting place has no soul. It makes no sense. It loses all its attraction—it is not a real resting place, with its warm meals, its talk, its leisure between two stages of a journey, its dreams and well-sheltered sleep.

Until that day, I had not known fire, real fire, outdoor fire. I had seen only tame fires, fires that were captive to a stove, obedient fires lit by a weak match, fires whose flames are confined. We limit them; we kill them; we bring them back to life. In other words, we degrade them. They are merely useful. And if we did not need them to heat and cook, we would no longer see them among us. But here, out in the wind, surrounded by reeds and willows, our fire was real fire, the ancient fire of primitive camps.

Such fires are not easily lit.

We found a gun flint in the boat. But no tinder. Gatzo

twisted some fibers of dead bulrushes and, by dint of patience, finally picked out a spark. We blew on it. Our hearts were pounding. We needed fire. Without fire, it was impossible to live as we had hoped.

At long last, the fiber crackled and we carried the flame to a pile of dried grasses. Placed under a cone of twigs, the burning grasses slowly set the twigs alight. We made some embers. We heated the oven and the stones. When the stones were burning hot, we put the fish, stuffed and dressed with fennel stalks, on top. The flesh sizzled. Scented with fire, fennel, and fresh oil, it was the best meal of my life. We drank some water. We dunked our biscuits in strong coffee. Then we stretched out on our backs and slept.

As for the fire, we kept it going under a tightly packed dome of ash. It was safe in its hole, where it gently thrived, invisible. It was simply a seed of fire buried in clay, but it lasted until evening, when we fed it again. Every now and then, it gave off a faint thread of smoke, and the smell of warm ash spread through the reeds that sheltered our camp.

From the start, we worried about hiding our smoke. Because the land, right nearby, was full of danger. Of course, the vegetation on our island hid us well, but the smoke escaped; at any moment it might betray our presence. The riverbanks looked deserted. But there are no deserted places where no one ever comes: an angler, a poacher, some aimless walker. We decided to explore the shore.

On the backwater, because the current was slight and the water shallow, we used a pole to navigate.

The land's borders were well protected. Amazingly vigorous water plants flourished there. We made our way slowly and carefully through wide, flowering prairies of fleawort and cotton grass, globeflower and swamp gladiolus. Our prow pushed aside duckweed and water lilies. Farther off, a dark channel was draped with marsh valerian. The watery expanse lay asleep beneath all these pink, white, yellow, and violet blooms—some raised up their stalks, others drifted on the still waters. We marveled at times when we came across tall blue gentians. And although they bloom only in September, we even saw a few water flags, sometimes called yellow iris.

We landed on a bed of gravel. After we had scaled the bank, we studied the countryside. It was empty.

"It is completely deserted," Gatzo said.

"Then we will be safe."

"Maybe, Pascalet. But we had better watch out. If we are the only ones around here, we will soon be discovered."

"By whom?"

"I do not know. Someone. There is always someone hiding."

A huge birch rose nearby. We climbed it. And then we looked out over the countryside.

Upstream, a vast valley. Woods shaded the low banks. In the distance a mountain that looked like a cloud. We could barely make it out.

Gatzo told me, "Last night, Pascalet, we covered a good twenty leagues. You can no longer see the island. We are in luck."

"Will they follow us?" I asked.

"They might. They need a boat."

"Mine is still stranded there, but it leaks."

"They will have it repaired soon. I know them. All they need is three days."

He thought, then spoke again. "Till then, we will be more or less safe. After that, we will see."

Downstream, a mile away, the backwater joined the river, which descended, narrowing, toward some lovely hills.

There it met rocky cliffs, and we saw it rolling along, sparkling in the setting sun. Farther still, on a stretch of brown land, a wide expanse of water glittered. Evening was already raising great plumes of warm mist. Some shimmered golden; others, steaming in the shadow of the hills, were already turning blue.

Right below us, extending along the backwater, ran a bare heath, enlivened only by stands of viburnum and tamarisk. Everywhere else was barren earth, stony. No life, not a single cabin. Only a meadow pipit or a lonely tree creeper here and there.

The heath rose rapidly in the South toward the crest of a bare hill that hid the countryside beyond us.

"There must be a village over there," Gatzo said.

"Where?"

"Somewhere behind that crest."

"How do you know?"

He smiled. "I can feel it. That is all. One day we will go there. And then you will see."

I admired Gatzo's self-assurance. He knew everything.

From above we could see a ribbon of bright grass cutting across the stony heath. It went down toward the backwater; here and there, a tuft of reeds sprayed out from it.

"A spring," Gatzo told me. "We should go see."

We went.

All we found under the high grass was some damp earth. We returned to the boat to fetch a pick.

"Let us dig here, Pascalet," Gatzo said.

We made a hole near a bulge in the clay. Water was seeping through. We continued to dig and fashioned a little basin. Through a breach in the clay, the water moistened a bed of sand. We flattened one side of our hole and stuck in a hollow reed. At first the reed stayed dry. We were aching with impatience, even more than for the fire. At long last, a droplet formed and grew round; for a long time, it hung, uncertain. Suddenly it fell. Another drop came, and slowly, at the tip of the green reed, the spring was born. It was barely a trickle, but out it oozed.

After an hour, the basin had collected a cup of clear water. Flat on our bellies, we each drank a mouthful. It still tasted sweetly of fresh clay and elderberry root.

I collected a bottleful. The boat returned us to our island, which we reached before nightfall.

The fire was stirred up, but carefully, because as soon as a flame escaped, the trees above vividly reflected its glow in their foliage.

The croaking frogs announced the night.

It was a calm one.

The days that followed were like the first day, the nights like the first night. Within us and all around us was a great peace. After the rapture of the first hours, we attuned our life to the life of these still waters. We regulated all our actions by the sun and the wind, by our hunger and thirst. And our hearts were wondrously full.

Everything we did lasted a long time, and we found this time too short. Because on the still waters, all movements are slow, and a boat moves slowly from one islet to the next. You live without impatience, and your days are long. You love them for their length and for their seeming monotony. But when you know how to look, nothing is more alive than these places where the air and the water seem to sleep.

Of course, there are times when they lie at rest, but underneath, a thousand unseen lives secretly continue to animate them.

I understood that then, and I have never been able to forget it since.

It was day, usually, that immobilized the layers of air and water.

As soon as the morning breeze withdrew, earth and water fell into stillness.

Toward eleven, Gatzo would take a big plunge. He would dive down slantwise until he reached some dark algae. Vaguely terrified, I would follow his dark body with my eyes, watching as it roved far from me, through those depths with their dangerous grasses. I would watch as he slowly folded and unfolded his long legs in that green wave. He would move through it for a long time, with such ease he seemed to have been born for water as much as for earth. To me, then, he became a troubling underwater creature, and I was startled when I saw him emerge, eyes closed, face solemn under his streaming hair, ten feet from the heavy boat where, unable to follow, I had waited in fear.

He would go to the bank to dry off. His bronze skin gently steamed in the full sun.

Not knowing how to swim, I never joined him. Sometimes, when he swam across the channels, I was afraid he would disappear. "If he does not come back, if he drowns, what will I do all by myself?" I worried.

The boat was too heavy for me alone, and I had no experience of this wild, free life he seemed so accustomed to.

Afternoons were hot. We would doze off. Aside from the whir of an insect or the surprising leap of a carp, nothing interrupted the silence.

On our islet, we dozed off comfortably in the shade of the reeds and dwarf birches. Sometimes, we hid the boat in a tunnel of greenery. Red willow and the "silver tree," so like an olive, grew there. We would tie up to a willow root and, carefree until nightfall, give in to the pleasure of watching butterflies, mayflies, and dragonflies flutter above the water. Or we would watch tireless pond skaters as they restlessly rowed, solely, it seemed, for the pleasure of rippling the water.

We spoke little. Gatzo would break the silence only to whisper, "Pascalet, keep still, there is an animal."

We did not move.

A tuft would stir. Most often, apart from this rustling, nothing betrayed the animal's presence. It remained invisible. Sometimes a pointed muzzle would poke through the reeds and an animal would appear, reddish brown, with a cruel eye—a weasel.

After cautiously sniffing the water, it would retreat into the underbrush.

Reassured by our silence, a dormouse would slip onto the bank, anxious, snooping. It never stayed long.

A teal or a coot would cross the channel and slip into the bulrushes, barely disturbing the water.

Sometimes, under the arching branches, a kingfisher would shoot out like an arrow, skimming the waves with its blue belly.

Soon, from the land, evening came to our retreat. All around us, the waters turned pink, gold, and hyacinth, and reddish leaves were reflected on the calm channel's smooth surface.

With little strokes of the pole, we left, going back over the wide-open water to spend the night.

We would cast our small anchor one and a half fathoms deep. We felt safe there, afraid as we still were of the shore.

We ate two biscuits and three dried figs in the prow of the boat and watched the night fall.

When night, with its mass of stars, had fully arrived, Gatzo dropped his guard and spoke to me a bit. The darkness brought us together.

"There must be an otter nearby," he would say.

"Where?"

"In the alders. It comes to drink. I hear it every night."

"Late?"

"Yes, very late."

"And you are awake?"

"It wakes me. It makes a lot of noise in the water when it is done drinking. It is a strong creature."

"I would like to see it," I told him.

"How can we see it? There is no moon."

And there was no moon, except for a faint crescent that grazed the horizon at dusk, then disappeared. Our nights were an empire of stars.

They hung on all sides, their interlaced silver limbs sparkling high above us in the darkness, while all around us, their thousands of pure flames shone on the still waters. Outside of time and space, we drifted between two calm skies.

Whole clans of frogs croaked, sometimes fiercely.

Later, not far from us, a gentler tribe of toads would sing. I loved them. Everywhere, plants and waters, shorelines and trees, came alive at nightfall with a confused, mysterious life. A duck would flap its wings in the reeds; an owl would screech on a black poplar; a brutal badger would rummage in a bush; a weasel, gliding from branch to branch, would cause two or three leaves to tremble lightly; a roving fox would yelp in the distance.

"It is a sad animal," Gatzo told me. "It is thinking."

I did not understand at all.

"Is that why it is sad, Gatzo?"

But Gatzo did not answer. He simply said, "It has lost its paradise. That is what our people say. The old folks know. But listen . . ."

I listened. Because a wondrous bird was beginning to sing on shore. Every night at the same time, atop the same elm, its courting call would rise over the waters and the country-side. It was the end of April, mating season, and the night-ingale's song was so beautiful the fox fell silent and we held our breath.

We fell asleep listening to it. Our sleep on those nights was light, so light we woke up several times before dawn.

Often, as we emerged from sleep, we would hear the voice of that wondrous bird, still singing. But now it was slower and more severe. Simply from the way its call echoed, alone, deep in the night, above the silence of unseen waters, we sensed that all the wetland creatures were at rest. We ourselves would fall back asleep, trailing after us for a long time that aching, lonely song.

At dawn, all we would see at first was a tall bird. On a narrow strip of silt, it would be standing completely still, some fifty yards from the boat. Its sharp beak threatening the water, high up on its legs, with its craw forward. It was a gray heron. We watched it excitedly, but silently, since herons take fright at the smallest thing.

Sometime later, a flock of mergansers would appear, always swimming out from a channel. It was a little morning flotilla, easily crossing the wide expanse of water, where a fine mist drifted. The ducks' appearance signaled the start of the morning. When they were twenty yards from shore, they swerved away as one, and, with the sun at their backs, the squadron set sail toward one of those leafy tunnels, where soon it disappeared in the half shadow.

Then all the animals stirred. It was time to wake.

And so we lived, thoughtless and carefree.

Sometimes everything was so calm that the calm weighed on us. Then we invented imaginary dangers.

"We do not know," Gatzo would say quietly, "what kind of people live here. Because there are people here."

"Of course there are," I repeated like an echo. "Perhaps they are savages."

I felt a shiver down my back, a delightful shiver. Just think! Savages!

Gatzo, cautious, nodded. "That bank over there, Pascalet, I have never trusted it."

He pointed to the backwater's left bank, covered in dense thickets.

"Imagine," he went on, "that we are among headhunters, cannibals. It is no different. All brush here, all brush there."

Then I would feel a mock terror. I enjoyed it. Because when you scare yourself through make-believe, you know well enough that you are not in any danger, but still you are afraid. It is one of the most delicious pleasures.

"Pascalet," Gatzo announced one fine morning, "we need to make some weapons!"

He fashioned a bow taller than he was. We made arrows from reeds.

The second a bush so much as stirred, we let an arrow fly.

When you have a weapon, you always end up using it. You shoot just for the sake of shooting. And it is a shame, but no one likes to shoot at nothing. You soon seek a target. I know of none more tempting than a handsome bird. Thousands of birds flocked around us, friendly, trusting. Seeing that we were harmless, they allied themselves to us, almost as much as to their fellows—peaceful, easy.

Often Gatzo, bow in hand, would closely observe a mallard that, fifteen feet from us, strutted on the water, dove, smoothed its feathers, even fell asleep with its beak under a wing, completely trusting.

Eyeing the bird, his finger tense, Gatzo would make the string vibrate then gently pull it back, as if unconsciously.

Then he would angrily raise the weapon and let the arrow fly randomly toward the shore.

In the evening, we would go to our lookout by the spring.

"Let us wait for night, Pascalet," Gatzo would say. "We will see wild beasts. They come at night to drink. I have seen their claw marks."

He showed them to me. These claws greatly troubled us both. But the beast did not appear. Well, we thought we saw it in the middle of the heath. It looked huge. We kept quiet.

"I was not dreaming, Pascalet," Gatzo swore, "I heard the sound of its feet."

"And I, Gatzo—I saw it wiggle its ears."

That night, we were no longer lying to ourselves. Yes, it was hard to see, but we definitely saw a shape, far away, in the middle of the heath. It appeared and disappeared mysteriously.

If I had not really seen it wiggle its ears as I insisted, at least I thought I had seen it, which allowed me to say, as if to settle the matter, "Gatzo, this beast is a monster."

Once back in our boat, we discussed it for a long time. The monster took shape. We gave it paws and a terrible tail. Why a tail? I do not know. Perhaps because of lions and tigers—because it was definitely a meat-eater.

"And yet, Gatzo, we did not see the glow of its eyes."

"He closed them, my poor Pascalet. He closed them just to trick us."

"Do you think so, Gatzo?" I asked, intrigued by this wonderful discovery.

Protectively, Gatzo assured me, "Pascalet, these animals are evil to the core."

I was excited, rapt with delight.

We talked a while longer, in order to settle the nature, breed, and name of the beast as precisely as we could. Neither a dog nor a wolf, we did not want that. Now that we were dealing with a real monster, we were not going to foolishly trade it in for some creature everybody knows about. We could not identify it, but then Gatzo had a thrilling idea.

"It is a Racal," he announced. "We will call it a Racal. There are Racals in the land. You saw a Racal. Nothing simpler."

Nothing, in fact, was simpler. The beast was a Racal, and even a huge Racal, the size of a donkey—and hence a dangerous Racal; what is more, a wandering Racal, a loner, one of those sensitive Racals irritated by the slightest thing, that charge you with a tremendous leap—the infamous leap of the Racal, surpassing that of the tiger. Clearly, this Racal must be ravaging the heath, where not one animal lived, not one plant grew. Because the Racal is solitary and rules the desert, it turns so ferocious when it grows old that even fighting bulls and buffaloes flee from it. The Racal is not hunted, because its flesh is as tough as leather and a wounded Racal is a terrifying enemy. Since the Racal roams only at night, it is not well known. Moreover, in our land, Racals were growing rare. Soon, none would be left. We had probably seen one of the last Racals of the era. And we stood there, panting with pleasure and fear.

"Gatzo!" I proclaimed, thrilled by the grandeur of our adventure, "we must return to the lookout."

And so the next night we returned to the lookout, but took our post in a tree.

"The Racal does not climb," Gatzo assured me. Gatzo knew better than I, for sure.

We remained perched on the main branch of an elm for half the night.

But the Racal did not return.

"He smelled us," Gatzo said.

Because everyone knows the Racal has an amazing sense of smell.

Two days later it gave us a real fright.

Around ten at night we heard the din of branches cracking in the thickets on shore. The brush trembled, branches snapped everywhere. Rough pawing roiled the water. Then the beast puffed, sniffed, grunted, snorted.

"It is taking a bath, Pascalet," whispered Gatzo, who had crawled along the floor of the boat to reach me. "But whatever you do, do not move. I hear it can swim."

This time, I really was trembling in terror.

By and by, the beast departed.

We were silent. Little by little, sleep overcame me.

But Gatzo, braver than I, watched over the shoreline until dawn.

From that day on, we were gripped by anxiety. It was a strange feeling. We began to be afraid of really being afraid ... because we had heard that din in the night with our own ears. There was nothing imaginary about it. An animal had come to disturb the peace of our refuge, where we thought no animal lurked—except the wild Racal.

Of course, we told ourselves this unknown visitor could only be a Racal, but after all what did we know? What if it was not a Racal? What if it was in fact a real animal?

"We should change our mooring, Pascalet," Gatzo advised.

Toward evening, we quietly weighed anchor.

First, we made a brief stop on the islet.

We took aboard a bundle of dry wood along with our fire, which we religiously set in an earthen pot. We placed the pot under a bench on the boat's floor.

And then, having said goodbye to our old home, we left its sheltered beach.

We took off down a channel. Little by little, its two banks drew closer, becoming one of those mysterious leafy tunnels that disappear into an archipelago of islands among willows and calm reed beds. We brushed the reeds' leafy stems as we passed, and this rustling disturbed the hidden nests of sensitive plovers and teals, who, skimming the water, complained about us. As we moved ahead, the tunnel darkened. At the far end, a point of light shone. We steered slowly, silently.

The leaves brushed our faces, and irritable insects flew out and swirled around our cheeks. We emerged at last onto another expanse of water, completely screened off by reeds and trees.

This little lake was asleep. The evening light barely lit up the deserted expanse of water. Tall poplars surrounded it. Bunched tightly together against the daylight, their leaves formed a dark hedge. Some grew up almost from the level of the water in the shallower pools. Others barred the soft horizon, where a crystalline brightness still illuminated the sky. The shoreline was rocky. From a cliff on high, a thick wood of holly oaks slanted down from the hills and darkened the water. The water, everywhere clear and still, gave off the faintest glow. An island rested at the center of the lake.

We could see a small chapel there. The whole island was planted with tall, ancient-looking cypresses. The boat, still drifting, glided along without rippling the water, and the island came toward us, calm, ghostly. With night falling, it seemed an unreal shape, the improbable abode of silence. Not a sound issued from it. An extraordinary hush pervaded the grasses, the trees, and the whole watery expanse.

The boat, its momentum exhausted, came to a halt between island and shore. Drifting, we dropped anchor, awed by the place and the silence. We were so moved that we did not dare to speak during our meal.

I slept poorly. The night was haunted. Keeping silent ourselves, in this strange silent place, we came to sense something like the mute vibration of an unknown life: obscure sounds or sighs; farther off, a murmur; a hesitant step on the shore perhaps; the breath of an unseen creature; and, under the mirror of the calm waters, the mysterious movement of secret waters.

Someone came to the shore. It might have been midnight. Gatzo heard the footsteps, as did I, very clearly, by the cliff.

The next day, we visited the island.

A mossy path led to the chapel. You reached it through a low porch. Wind and rain had worn the soft stone façade. Its features seemed ancient, burnished by lichens and the sun's long labor.

Above the door was a carved niche with a little painted plaster Virgin. The colors had faded—we glimpsed some pink on the gown. An inscription in blue letters surrounded this humble image.

It announced the chapel's name, a beautiful name:

Our Lady of Still Waters.

The sanctuary was poor and looked abandoned. On the painted wood altar were two small lead candlesticks. A reed cross stood on the tabernacle. Against the whitewashed walls, a wreath of dried rushes and red osier still hung. The air smelled damp.

We left the chapel to look around. In back, Gatzo discovered two tombstones hidden in the high grass where blue speedwell was blooming.

Cypresses had grown up all around the chapel and the two tombstones.

The island was so small the water bathed the ancient roots

of those trees, whose stark shapes cast dark reflections in the water.

After the island, we explored the cliff and the wood of holly oaks, not daring to go deeper inland. That was where the heath began. Up a rocky slope, thickets of broom, rock-rose, and thorny holly crept up toward the rounded back of a hill, where a forest of pines advanced.

Not a soul. Not a house. In the sky, a sparrow hawk was gliding above us, pure.

I said, "This place is sad, Gatzo."

Gatzo said, "You are right. It is not like other places. There are spirits here."

Surprised, I asked him, "Who told you that?"

He whispered, "You heard it last night the same as I did, did you not? Stirring. What came here was a ..."

I said, "Yes, I heard it. Are you sure it is a spirit?"

"No, Pascalet. But we can find out. If we hide tonight it will probably come back."

My heart was pounding.

Gatzo went on. "The moon goes down around ten. It is pitch-black out. There is a big hollow at the foot of the cliff. We will lie in wait there."

I was frightened. He sensed it right away. "Pascalet," he said, "we have got to see. We are not children."

I was silent. He went on, "We have not been traveling for nothing ... Stay if you wish ... I will go by myself."

I was ashamed; but my fear grew so strong I replied, "What you are doing is forbidden; you will be punished."

He shrugged and remained silent until after the moon had set.

Then he undressed, placed his clothes on his head, slipped into the water, and swam to the cliff. I could see him moving about on the shore. He was probably putting his clothes back on. Then he vanished.

The boat was resting near the island. Hidden by the shadow of the trees, it could not be seen from shore.

I was sitting on the forward bench. From there I had a good view of the shoreline.

Nothing was stirring there.

The wait was long, but I had no wish to sleep. I wanted to see the thing too, if only from a distance.

It was about midnight when it came.

The spirit walked along the shore, pushed aside a shrub, and went down to the strand. To me it looked like a little speck of white. This speck of white roamed around a bit, then approached the water.

That is when I lost my head. I unmoored the boat and gently pushed off with the pole. The boat obeyed me and began to slip through the ink-black water. "It is so dark out," I thought, "the spirit will not see me. It is impossible. If I can see it, it is because it is white." Despite this whiteness, I could not make it out. Did it have a shape? I was moving toward it, but motionless on the strand, it was still just a bright spot in the shadow. Lost in that shadow, it probably failed to see me slowly drawing near. Suddenly, it let out a faint cry—I had just appeared near the bank.

I could hear it crying out, "My God! It is a spirit!" I was surprised to be taken for a spirit, but I regained my composure and spoke up. "And you, what is your name?"

The spirit fled, but Gatzo, leaping from his hiding place, caught it on the run.

"I have got it," he exclaimed. "It is a girl! Just think!"

The boat scraped up on the strand. I joined Gatzo.

He was holding the girl by the wrists. She did not resist. She looked about our age, but we could not see her clearly.

"What are you doing here? Who are you? Where do you live?"

Gatzo bombarded her with questions. She was silent, but she did not seem to be afraid of us.

"We will not hurt you," Gatzo declared, more gently.

He released her wrists. Then she said, "I know you. You are the ones who came to the backwater about a week ago. They are looking for you in all the villages."

I froze with fear. But Gatzo calmly asked, "Really? They are looking for us? Who?"

"Here in Pierrouré it is the village constable."

"And how does that work? Tell us."

"Every morning at eleven he beats the drum and makes an announcement. Then he goes home. That is how it has been for four days. Everybody knows about you."

"So, we can sleep in peace. You will not say a word, will you?"

"I will not say a word," the girl replied. "But there is someone else looking for you too. And he will know how to track you down."

Now Gatzo was worried.

"What is he like?"

"A tall, rough man, with dark skin. He came by the river on an old wreck of a boat."

Terrified, I was thinking, "It must be Bargabot. We are done for."

The girl went on. "He has been here since last night. He showed up at the same time as the marionettes."

"What marionettes?" Gatzo asked. His voice was trembling.

"The little theater. Tomorrow they will put on a show under the elm. They come every year. They perform at night after dinner. The same troupe always comes. Last year there were two people. This year there is only one old man, all alone."

She was silent. Gatzo was also silent.

Suddenly she said, "I have to go back."

We went with her as far as the woods. She walked in front. She could see in the dark as well as Gatzo. At the edge of the woods, we said goodbye.

It was so dark under the trees that even Gatzo was surprised by the girl's fearlessness.

"Why do you come down to the water at night?" he asked her.

She held her tongue, but Gatzo kept questioning her, gently insistent. At last she responded to his soft voice.

Her parents were dead. She had been taken in when she was very little. She worked for good people, grandfather Saturnin and grandmother Saturnine. They had one grandson, Constantin, twelve years old. One day, the three of them went away on a long journey. They had left her alone in the house, with an old servant who never stopped scolding. It was said that they had gone to live far away, in a sad land. God alone knew why. And there, naturally, they had grown sad too. But they did not dare return home. And so she came secretly at night to pray to Our Lady of the Waters to bring them back to the village, where everyone missed them.

This story pained us deeply. As she told it, the girl herself seemed pained. When she came to the end, she was crying.

Moved, Gatzo asked, "What is your name, little one?"

"Hyacinth," she answered, and continued to cry.

Just then we heard a footstep in the pine forest. A strange footstep, an animal's footstep.

Frightened I said, "It is the beast! The Racal!"

The girl said, "Not at all. It is my donkey. He has come to get me."

We saw a shadow. The beast emerged from the darkness.

The girl called it. "Come, my dear Trousers. Easy now. You must not scare them this time."

The donkey came. He was dressed quite wonderfully.

"It is the countryside's enchanted donkey," Hyacinth told us.

She might have been laughing.

Suddenly, she grew sad.

"I will not be back tomorrow. I want to see the little theater. They will perform for the children in the village square. There is a moon, every night."

Gatzo and I were silent.

Then Hyacinth mounted her donkey, and the two of them plunged into the woods as naturally as can be.

The next day dragged by. We wandered around but felt no pleasure. Until then, everything had interested us—a bird, a fly, a frog, a butterfly. Now, for no reason, we were bored. Gatzo kept to himself. He barely spoke. Again, he wore that inscrutable face I did not like. His vacant look was a wall between us. I felt alone. My heart heavy, I was silent.

Toward the end of the afternoon, I could no longer stand it. The boat was moored under the cliff. I leapt ashore and went for a walk.

It was very hot under the oaks, but the light was lovely, and little reddish-brown squirrels, not at all alarmed, studied me from on high.

Their friendship made me happy, and carefree as we are at that age, I forgot my sorrow as I walked through the woods where blue wood pigeons and black-winged golden orioles calmly flew from one tree to the next.

Farther up in the foliage, other birds were singing. The woods climbed up toward high hills; soon a big stretch of countryside lay under my command. I stopped and sat on a rock.

Toward the West, rather far away, the river reappeared, shining. On a large flatboat, two small men were slowly fishing with a cast net. To my left, holly oaks and tall pines scaled the slopes of the first hills. Although dusk was carving blue valleys and purple ravines into these hills, their peaks remained sunlit.

Beyond the shoulder of one hill, I could see a bit of village—five or six houses, a tower, a small steeple. Beyond the steeple, three or four plumes of smoke. That is where the main part of the town must be hiding. Halfway up the hillside, I could see the path that led to it. The land was deserted, but a donkey was walking along the path. A solitary donkey, without a driver. Still, it was following the trail precisely, carrying two side baskets. It was coming toward me with small steps, as if it knew exactly where it was going.

"Oh," I thought, quickly realizing, "it is Hyacinth's donkey. Soon I will see it more clearly."

I waited, my heart pounding. But the donkey suddenly veered to the right and disappeared under the pines.

Almost immediately, night began to fall. At first I did not notice.

By the time I snapped out of it, it was already quite dark. I hurried back to the mooring.

The boat was still there, but Gatzo was gone.

4. THE PUPPETEER OF SOULS

FOREVER.

I was sure of it immediately. But I did not want to believe it. Which is why I waited.

"He will come back," I told myself, not really believing it. "He must have gone snooping around a rabbit hole. It was a mistake to have left him alone. He got bored." But he did not come back, and little by little I lost faith that he would. To console myself I hoped against hope. And yet it was useless. I knew very well he was gone.

Everything told me I was alone—the animals and their sounds, the waters and their silence. Everything. The sad little frog croaking in its clump of watercress at the far end of a lagoon—it too was alone. As was the big-headed owl hidden away among the leaves of a huge poplar on the other shore, periodically complaining to another owl close by, perched on a cypress in the middle of the island. This cypress-dweller replied patiently and mournfully to its melancholy companion, and back and forth went their lugubrious conversation across the lonely marshes. Though no sound came from the perfectly peaceful waters to darken my heart, the marshes spoke to me with their stillness. They were silent, and so I knew I was alone.

I should have been afraid, but I believe that my sorrow at having been abandoned blunted my fear. I was on edge even so. Vague perils menaced me—sounds, a shadow, a small something that breathed.

When the moon rose, my sorrow grew. Seeing the deserted expanse of marshes in the moonlight, I discovered the vastness of my solitude. I was so alone that, although deep within myself I was calling out to Gatzo, not a sound came from my mouth. I was terrified at how my voice would echo in this watery wasteland.

"He is in the village," I told myself. "But how could he have gone there without me?"

Because it was the thought of Gatzo's betrayal that bothered me, more than my being all alone at night in such a wild place. By leaving, he had shattered the most beautiful friendship of my life. It hurt me terribly. Because I would never again find a companion like him—a companion who was stronger, smarter, braver than I was. He was my first friend.

A dark foreboding made me secretly fear that he would never come back. Desperate, I decided to quit this sad mooring where I was so alone and go look for him.

I thought he might be in the village where I had seen those few houses at sunset.

I remembered the path the donkey had taken. By cutting through the oaks, it could be easily reached. The full moon lit up the edge of the woods, and I headed toward them.

That night the moon helped me a great deal—its brightness lit my way, and soft and vast, it calmed me down, casting a spell. For the moon is the most enchanting of heavenly bodies. Its light is so close! We feel its attention, its affection, and during the full moons of spring, its fond friendship softens the whole countryside. For children who wake during the night, there is no more charming comforter. Through the open window, it lights up their rooms, and when they fall back asleep, it bestows the most beautiful dreams on their slumbers.

I must have had one of those dreams.

Of course, I was not asleep in my room. But how could everything I did that night—that I saw, and supposed I heard—have taken place so easily if it were not all in a dream?

The entire oak forest was bathed in the blue rays of the lunar light coming down through the black leaves. The branches of those old trees were all steeped in astral blue. And when I myself stepped out of the darkness into one of those bright spaces, I was immediately transformed into a little body of molded moonlight.

I crossed the woods easily, and soon the path appeared. I was not seeking it, it arrived on its own, naturally flooded with light. And right away it seemed so friendly I surrendered to its gentle allure. It was a beautiful nighttime path, one of those paths that keeps you company, that you can talk to, and that shares its little secrets along the way. You tread such paths calmly, fearlessly. They have remained innocent through and through and would not know how to lead you astray. Time no longer matters, and space melts warmly away into the nighttime pleasure of walking, walking. You never know where you are coming from or where you are going, when you left or when you will arrive—but do you ever arrive? These paths never come to an end, and if by some chance they leave you behind, it is to gently drop you in an even more magical place.

And I, who am telling you all this, ought to know. That is just where my path dropped me.

It seemed to have been put on these hillsides solely in order to lead me to the most remarkable village in the world.

Was it even in this world? It was hard to believe, unlikely and unreal as everything there seemed. Many times on that strange night, I was simpleminded enough to imagine it had been created by innocent fairies for the delight of dreamy, fanciful children, just outside of paradise.

I entered the village from above. The narrow streets were deserted. The houses seemed empty. And yet they smelled of warm bread and spelt soup. Clearly, the people had just left. And now there was not a sound, not a lamp.

Even the dogs, so ferocious on the outskirts of villages, had gone off with their masters. The chickens were asleep. There was not even a cat. They had taken themselves elsewhere.

I followed a little sloping street, past silent house after silent house, until suddenly I found myself in a little square.

And the whole mystery was revealed.

The village was there, the whole village, human and animal. And it seemed to be waiting.

It seemed to be waiting confidently. It was a patient, honest village. You could tell, just by looking at the people. They were sensible and calm; there were several rows of them.

The first row sat soberly on a wooden bench. At the center reigned the mayor.

The mayor was clean shaven and had straight white hair. He wore his Sunday best. A huge, starched collar rose from his puce jacket, and it must have bothered him a lot, because he did not dare turn his head. Very patiently, he looked straight ahead, which gave him great dignity as mayor.

Sensing his stillness, the others kept still too, out of respect. Immediately to his right sat the old priest. From habit, his hands were crossed on his stomach, and for this occasion his fat red face had taken on a kind, resigned look.

Beside him, the notary, a little old man, thin as a rail, with a mocking mouth. He was scratching the tip of his pointy nose.

The potbellied doctor, in an alpaca jacket, a straw boater on his head, wiped his gold-framed glasses with a checked handkerchief, the better to see. He too was an elderly man with a bearded, rosy face.

Just to the left of the mayor, the village constable was asleep. He seemed older than the world, but he sported a military goatee, and a silver braid encircled his kepi.

Beside him, a sturdily built old man sat proudly. His white beard spread out like a vast fan on his chest. From time to time, he raised a big fleshy nose to sniff the air; in his weather-beaten old face, the green eyes remained unmoving.

This was the old navigator, the pride of the village.

Plump, mustachioed, and angry, the little tobacconist hid under the navigator's shoulder. In his sixties and retired, he was the only one in the row who was not always kindhearted.

Such was the bench of dignitaries.

Behind them were the ordinary villagers.

First the women, in three groups. To the right, all the grandmothers; in the center, all the married women. Huddled together on the left were the young girls, who never stopped laughing or whispering.

Behind the women stood four groups of men. There were tall ones and wide ones, some with mustaches and some clean shaven. But all their faces wore the same set look of calm and powerful simplicity.

They were all gazing in the same direction, at a huge elm whose foliage spread like a dome over the square.

On the tree's lowest branches hung an array of little lights and large, multicolored Venetian glass lanterns.

Under the elm stood a modest canvas theater. And on either side of this theater, in plain sight, right in front of the dignitaries, the children were lined up on school benches—the boys to the right, the girls to the left. They were waiting as calmly as the grownups.

The little theater's curtain had not yet been raised. But we admired the painting on it. It portrayed a donkey. The donkey sat in an armchair. He wore glasses and was holding a book. In front of him, a little boy knelt and listened. The donkey was teaching him. Above the donkey and child, an ivy-crowned mask with lowered eyes smiled maliciously and indulgently.

Behind the theater was a church with a deep porch all in shadow.

Above the church, the shadow, the theater, the villagers, the lanterns, and the huge oak floated the great sky of the April moon, all ablaze.

I do not know what happened first, not really. I was too rapt to take it in, and perhaps such a marvelous sight had been created expressly to enchant eyes and ears.

First we heard, from behind the theater, a quavering voice, charming and rich with wisdom. Immediately, I was touched to the bottom of my heart. The voice described what was being prepared behind the curtain. It spoke the names of the characters and asked us to believe in them, because they would laugh for us, cry, hate, love—in other words, live and die like humans.

After this little speech, the curtain rose on a garden and

its gardener. In this garden grew huge fruit. The gardener was very proud of this fruit, so proud that he scorned all other gardeners. He had a young wife and a son as handsome as the day is long. We saw the two of them running under the trees to catch big blue butterflies. The gardener was almost as proud of his wife and son as of his melons and plums. Which is why he forbade them to visit the little neighboring gardens, and they obeyed.

One day a beggar came by, an old beggar haggard with hunger and thirst. A peach hung over the path, on the other side of the garden hedge. The beggar plucked it and prepared to eat. Suddenly, the proud gardener appeared. Red with anger, he jumped on the beggar—poor man—making him drop the fruit with a blow of his staff. The fruit fell onto the path and the beggar, resigned, departed without complaint.

Now, you should know that this beggar was Saint Théotime, who was traveling on business—in other words, on the business of the Good Lord.

The scene changed, and the Good Lord Himself arrived on a cloud. He was very angry and spoke to the gardener so harshly that everyone in the audience, especially the girls, trembled with fear. Then he too left, growling threats, while behind the theater a drumroll imitated thunder. The Good Lord, enraged, was going to avenge his Saint.

Then we were back to the earthly garden. The child was playing. You could see him running without a care in the world while, just below Théotime's peach tree, an old witch watched him with burning eyes. She had picked up the fruit from the path.

Oh! What a beautiful fruit! I can still see it. Having licked it, the witch placed it, pink and tender, at the foot of the tree.

The child passes by, sees it, eats, and drops into a faint. The witch falls on him and carries him into the air.

Years go by. We see a camp of Gypsies. That is where the child is living now. He has grown a lot, but because the witch poisoned the fruit, he has lost his memory. He left behind all of his recollections the moment he bit into the peach. And he is no longer good-natured. He is now the worst scoundrel in the tribe. He lies, he swears, he cheats, he steals—as naturally as breathing. And for no reason at all, he grabs his knife. Everyone is afraid of him.

And his parents?

Having lost his memory, he forgot them long ago. But *they* remember. And they are very sad. The fruits on the trees grow as big and as abundantly as before, but all in vain—the gardener no longer even thinks about picking them. He has grown old. Just imagine it: he hides from his wife and cries all night long.

His grief has turned his hair white; he no longer harbors an ounce of pride in his breast.

Yet he and his wife still hope.

"The little one will come back," they think. And they wait.

The door is open night and day, so he can enter the house without calling out.

And then one night the Gypsies arrive. They hide in the woods.

Now, that very same night, an old beggar comes asking for alms. He is hungry and thirsty. The gardener remembers. He gives him a basket of peaches. The beggar takes only one peach and bites into it but does not eat it. Then he tells the gardener, "Remember to keep this peach at the head of your

bed, and be patient. One day someone will come to eat it."
After that, he vanishes. It was Saint Théotime.

The Gypsies, hidden in the dark wood, see the lovely
garden. All together, they declare, "The gardener is rich. We
will rob him." And when they draw straws to see who will
be the robber, the skillful child draws the short straw.

The moon sets, night falls, the owl hoots, and the child
threads his way through the garden. He reaches the house,
finds the door, and with his fingers seeks the lock. But his
hands meet only emptiness. This strange house, unafraid of
robbers, sits there with its door wide open in the middle of
the night.

The rascal hesitates, trembles.

Still he gets on with it, out of pride. But he is hot, his
throat burns, he is dying of thirst. Suddenly he is in a room.
An old man is asleep on his back. A night-light illumines
his face. And beside him, by his pillow, on a painted dish, is
a perfectly juicy peach, where it looks like two teeth have
left their mark.

The robber child stretches his hand toward the fruit and
brings it to his mouth. What flavor! What sweetness! But
it is not a fruit. It fills your whole body, it tugs at your soul.
Where am I? . . . He cries out.

The good old man wakes up. His wife comes running.

Oh! It is their son. He is here, he sees them, he remembers,
he weeps.

The Good Lord appears on his cloud and nods, satisfied.

The curtain falls.

In those days, in our villages, people were still artless, and
when they were delighted they were fully delighted. Their

artlessness let them immediately grasp a tale's deep meaning. And if the tale's simplicity enraptured them, it is because that simplicity reflected their own wisdom. Reduced to a handful of simple thoughts, this wisdom might seem poor to us, yet it is a treasure distilled from age-old experience.

This true knowledge, if truly alive, is never bleak. It makes itself known and inspires our imagination. And so it becomes, as in this tale, an entertainment, and what it teaches is so lovely that its wisdom enchants us.

Clearly it enchanted everyone in the village that night. All through the performance, the mayor sat with his mouth wide open. The priest himself gaped at the angels and made the sign of the cross when the Good Lord appeared. The notary and the doctor declared themselves satisfied. In his rage, the navigator almost got up four times to strangle the hateful witch and the treacherous Gypsies. It was hard to hold him back. Whole rows of villagers voiced strong feelings. "Ho's!" and "ha's!" quietly rumbled, betraying anger, scorn, pity. The children said nothing, but they stared strangely wide-eyed. They were hypnotized by the drama. A magician had caught them in his web of charms. They were no longer just watching; they had moved from audience to stage, where they were no longer themselves but the beings they saw there. The play was not being acted for them—it was they who, miraculously, acted it themselves. Lined up on their benches, they could be seen to sigh all at once, their intent little faces tightly pressed together, enraptured, completely still.

One little girl's face especially. She had pink cheeks, a wide mouth, and very green eyes. Her hair was red and neatly combed. A little pigtail was tied straight back on her neck. There could be no doubt it was Hyacinth. Just from the look of terror and delight that seemed to transfix her face, you could tell: no other child had been as captivated by the performance as she was. Her whole soul had been in it.

The curtain fell; a great silence followed. Then the same quavering voice spoke from behind the stage.

"Good people," it said, "the show is over. Now my dog Piquedou will come around with a bowl between his teeth. He will be taking up a collection. Be good to him. He is my only companion on the road. For my children are no longer in this world, and, as in the fable, I had a grandson, but he was stolen by Gypsies. I have been making the marionettes dance throughout the countryside for fifty years. After me, no one will come with them again. This is the last time you will see them, my friends. I am growing very old, and I will not be returning to the village. Tonight, then, I say farewell. And now, when the dog comes around, give us a penny for the theater."

And so the village cried. The women blew their noses, the men wiped their eyes, and the mayor sneezed. Then all together the girls lifted their voices and said, "Grandfather Savinien, please come out one more time!"

The curtain moved and a head appeared. It was large and bald, but a crown of beautiful white hair fell around the shining pate, blending with the old man's long beard, which flowed down like snow. His eyes were clear and open, and when, with difficulty, the old man stood up, three hundred faces softened tenderly.

He was wearing an old redingote with a scarf around his neck. You could tell he was very poor and very patient.

So poor and so patient that, on seeing him emerge from his hiding place so simply and with such gracious courtesy, the whole village, seized with respect, fell silent. Not that he was smiling or trying to please; his old face was marked by its unaffected purity of expression.

When he was fully upright, we heard someone sobbing in the leafy branches overhead.

It was coming from low in the elm. Everyone looked up. And so Gatzo was discovered. Astride a branch, he was crying. He was crying and he was furious with himself. He was ashamed to be crying with three hundred sensible people below, all of them stunned to see him up there streaming with tears. But still he cried, and from below, his grandfather Savinien, struck dumb with emotion, stood staring at him blankly, utterly baffled that the lost child had fallen before him from the heavens.

"Come down, little one," cried the women. "We will give you some mulled wine."

The grandfather said nothing; emotion had stolen his voice. He was still staring at his grandson, whose legs dangled through the foliage. And Gatzo, from his branch on high, was staring at him and crying.

At the foot of the tree, the dignitaries—the mayor, the priest, the doctor—formed a circle and smiled at the child to encourage him to come down. Which he did.

"Gently," said the cautious grandmothers, "do not break your bones, you little madman."

And the men nodded and congratulated Grandfather Savinien.

"Look," they said, "how well he manages it. Agile as a squirrel!"

When, sliding down the trunk, Gatzo dropped to earth right in front of the mayor, everyone sighed "Ouf!" with relief.

Now, this was a good mayor. His name was Mathieu

Varille. They had never known such a good mayor in that part of the world. So no one was surprised when, turning to the crowd, he graciously announced, "The mulled wine is on me!"

A murmur of satisfaction arose from three hundred souls.

And the mayor said, "Let us go, my children! And in order—the little ones first; then the girls; after the girls, the women; and finally, all the men."

The village constable, now awake, picked up his drum and went to the head of the line.

The mayor took his place behind him. To his right was Grandfather Savinien. To his left, Gatzo, completely at ease. And the mayor held each of them by the hand.

Behind them, in a row, the five dignitaries: the priest, the notary, the doctor, the navigator, and the tobacconist.

The villagers followed, the little ones in front. In the first row you could see Hyacinth, with her blue eyes and pigtail. She was looking straight ahead, serious.

The old folks brought up the rear.

The village constable beat the drum softly with his old hands.

Ancient though they were, from the tips of his drumsticks came a cheerful marching tune. And everyone, without even realizing it, strutted to the bouncing rhythm.

And so I saw them all go by, their faces beaming. The girls, holding each other around the waist, sang happily and swayed.

"Never in fifty years," said the old women, "have we seen such a celebration."

The old men nodded their approval.

And the young people laughed without knowing why.

When the last row had gone by, I saw the dog. He followed with the bowl between his teeth and a look that said that this was what a dog ought to do. He followed, with his muzzle at the old men's heels, trotting along. And, although he was bringing up the rear, he was as satisfied as anyone.

He went by, and I was left by myself.

No one had noticed me, not even Gatzo. Gatzo respectfully held the mayor's solemn hand and seemed to be in awe by such an honor. Had he even seen me? He might not have seen anything that night, being king of the procession. But I had seen him and I loved him, and my heart was swollen with pain, my eyes were wet with tears.

Nothing remained of the festivities except the empty school benches and the little canvas theater with its donkey painted on the curtain.

One by one, the little lamps went out in the branches of the elm, and up above, in the milky sky, you could tell the moon was starting to sink behind the hills.

I felt so alone, so sad, I had no idea what to do.

Behind the abandoned theater, they had forgotten to put out a candle. It burned, flickering, the glow of its unseen flame spreading a faint and mysterious crown of light above the theater's flimsy roof.

I became fascinated and I was moving toward it when a lean man suddenly appeared beside the theater.

He was taller than the canvas roof, and casually leaning against the posts of the little structure, he began to carefully inspect every corner of the square.

He spied me. It was Bargabot!

But he did not bat an eye.

I fled.

5. PASCALET'S LONELINESS

I HARDLY know how I found my way to the mooring. As long as I was running or walking, I did not feel a thing. But no sooner had I reached the water's edge than a strange sense of silence and loneliness assailed me.

Nothing moved on the marshes, nothing in the air. The water was leaden. Damp shrouded the sad landscape, where a solitary star sparkled through the spiky reeds. The moon had gone to visit other worlds. Right in the middle of these melancholy waters, the island floated in darkness. I was too afraid to stay on the bank where the boat was moored. I untied it and, leaning on my heavy pole, pushed off from dry land.

"It is all over," I muttered to myself. "Might as well let the boat drift away."

But it barely drifted. That night, no current stirred the surface of the lifeless water. The boat, slipping away from the banks, floated in a sort of magical torpor, and soon the faint impulse driving it dwindled and died.

Wrapped in a blanket, I lay down at the bottom.

I waited to know my fate. I knew this was my last night of sleeping in the world of still waters. I wanted to sleep through it as I had those other nights, stretched out on my back on the floor of my boat, breathing the nighttime scent of fresh water through the planks. Despite the threat of dreams, I drew so much peace from it, and so much rest.

When I woke the sun was already high. Before I had opened my eyes, I knew someone was with me in the boat.

Above me I could smell steaming coffee, hot bread, and a joyous pipe.

"Bargabot," I said, my eyes still shut, "when do we sail?"

Bargabot spoke. "Soon. We will have some coffee and take off."

I rose.

In the prow, Bargabot, his long pipe in his mouth, was crouched in front of a stove—unearthed from who knows where—carefully pouring hot coffee into a big clay bowl.

"Come, my boy!" he cried. "It warms you and clears your head when you first get up."

He drank contentedly, reaching for the bread with his rough, coarse, manly hands, so deft at preparing meals.

The coffee roused my courage.

I asked, "Tante Martine, Bargabot?"

"She is waiting for you."

"Did she cry?"

"She cried."

This reassured me a great deal.

"Your father," he added, "will not be back until the end of the week."

"Praise God!" I thought.

Things might work out, it seemed. I grew braver. "Were you afraid for me, Bargabot?" I asked.

Stunned, Bargabot stared. "Goodness!" he said, and that was that.

His looks and his tone made me think that he was, all in all, happy enough with me.

But now he said it was time to go, which was when I finally noticed that while I slept we had changed moorings.

We were anchored elsewhere on the backwater now, separated from the mainstream only by a shallow lagoon. I could see the river clearly through the reeds, big, swift sheets of it flowing by.

A small skiff floated beside the boat's sturdy flank.

There was hardly anything to it: six planks, no bench, but two enormous oars, and—height of arrogance—a mast.

"Get in," Bargabot ordered. "We are leaving your old crake here. Too heavy to go up against this current. I will come back for it."

Reluctantly, I stepped into Bargabot's boat.

"Get in front," he told me.

I had to sit on the planks.

"A good breeze," he noted with satisfaction.

Then he hoisted the sail. It was old and patched, but filled by the wind, it flapped. And so the boat leaned toward the water that rose almost to the level of the gunnel, and we set sail.

Bare to his waist, Bargabot gripped the oars and rowed vigorously with both arms. The skiff sat so low to the water that several times waves splashed my elbows. I was afraid that, under the weight of the sail, we would capsize in the middle of the river. But the skiff held up. Bargabot, oars in his fists, wind at his back, faced the powerful river unconcerned. We cut through black whirlpools and, pitching and rolling, leapt head-on over the tumultuous water. Everything breathed joy—Bargabot, the airy waves, the stiff breeze, the sky striped with birds, and the great hazy estuary already sun-warmed and steaming in full morning between the water and the bright blue hills. I forgot my troubles a little and, intoxicated by the wild air flying madly over the river, surrendered to the pleasure of drinking the wind.

Toward noon, we stopped on the left bank to eat. Bargabot shot a duck. He had a huge punt gun, an ancient weapon that worked with a flint. When fired, it left a long trail of red sparks in the air, along with plenty of smoke smelling of saltpeter and fire.

We spent the night under a starry sky.

The next day we sailed as we had the day before, but closer to the banks, and in calm water.

Toward evening, the island came into view. Bargabot spoke little. But pointing to the island, he said, "It has been cleaned out, little one. They got scared." And he gently stroked his gun. He seemed pleased with himself.

"Is there nothing left?" I asked.

He shook his head and was silent. I sensed he was hiding something. But I did not dare question him.

We passed the island, veered, and gently came aground.

We reached the house just as night was falling.

We crossed the garden. Under the trellis on the terrace was a lighted lamp sitting on the table, which had been set. On the clean white tablecloth were three plates, a pitcher of water, and two jugs of clear wine. The bread, with its big knife, rested in a basket. The loaf was reddish. Through the open door, we caught a glimpse of the kitchen hearth, where two pans and two big pots simmered peacefully.

In front of the fire was Tante Martine. In an old armchair, in a white apron, her piqué bonnet tied under her chin, her hands at rest on her knees, solemn and still, she sat keeping watch over the evening meal. Her dark face expressed confidence. She was awaiting the lost child. Perhaps every evening she had lit this fire, prepared this meal, set this table, and hung this lamp under the trellis, without losing hope.

And now that I was here, she seemed, in front of this

fragrant food cooked for me with love, the very soul of the family home. Although I was too young at the time to understand such serious matters, the almost religious feeling that emanated from this faithful and attentive old kinswoman touched my heart.

And so I could not keep from bursting into tears. She heard me and, very gently, she called to me.

"Pascalet, come my child, let me kiss you."

Sobbing, I entered the kitchen.

Bargabot remained on the threshold, his gun in hand.

I let myself go on Tante Martine's breast. She called me tender names: "Good-for-nothing," "Drifter," "Sweetheart," I do not know what else. And we kissed each other fervently, in front of the fire and the pots, from which, as if to reassure me and move me even more, wafted the aromas of the meal that had probably been cooking since morning, sprinkled with thyme, stuffed with spices. And even as I cried, I was hungry.

We ate outdoors quite peacefully. And then I went to bed, while Tante Martine stayed up.

Bargabot left late. The two of them whispered together for a long time. They had put out the lamp, and they were speaking on the terrace.

From above, through the open window, I could hear their muffled voices like a murmur. No doubt they were speaking of me, and I dozed off thinking I could slumber without fear now that they sheltered my sleep.

My parents returned a week later. As you might imagine, Tante Martine said not a word about my escapade. Still, she complained a lot, in keeping with family custom, which demanded my parents feel sorry for her, especially after entrusting her with the household during their absence. They knew it was meaningless. As did she. But the sacred rituals of complaint and reproach were scrupulously observed.

Among the reasons for distress, I played my part.

"He suffered from insomnia the whole time," Tante Martine claimed. "He reads too much. It gets him all worked up."

"He does read too much," my father agreed, believing her.

And turning to me: "Pascalet, you need to have fun. At your age, you should be out having fun."

They took my pulse. It was racing. They made me stick out my tongue. It was white.

My mother worried.

"Nothing to worry about," my father said. "It is because he is always sitting!"

They took away my books and gave me some senna. I swallowed it reluctantly, but I had to go through with it. After all, it was not too high a price to pay.

To console me, Tante Martine brought out some honey cakes she had baked in secret.

Still, the administration of this laxative, far from perking me up, engendered, deep within me, a mysterious lassitude. Everyone had their own explanation. For my father, it was my liver. For my mother, my spleen. And for Tante Martine, my lungs. "He does not breathe well," she would say. "Listen to him carefully. Pascalet's just one long sigh these days." It is true I sighed a lot, perhaps out of lassitude, perhaps from something else. But I did not know any better than my family what the cause of my malaise was, it was so obscure.

And still it grew, and nothing became any clearer.

They gave me back my books. "After all," my father grumbled, "let him read them if he wants!" But I did not read them. They bored me.

We were entering the month of June. We passed from June to July, from fruits to harvest, through beautiful weather. Cool mornings, clear nights, soft sunshine, beautiful evenings. Even in August, summer warmed but did not scorch the countryside, where the springs never once dried up.

And still I languished. An undefinable boredom weighed me down. The days seemed long. With nothing to do, I wandered here and there, around the threshing floor, through the orchard, under the old plane trees.

Sometimes, tired of the house and its surroundings, I went to sit on the path, on the edge of the ditch. And there, without pleasure, I waited.

Without pleasure and without hope. I would have liked for someone to come by, anyone: the postman, an animal, a dog, a donkey perhaps.

Bargabot no longer visited the house. What had become of him? No one ever spoke of him. His absence went unnoticed. And yet it was especially during the warm months that he used to bring us fish once a week. Now no more Bargabot, and no one was concerned.

But I thought about him, and thinking about him often kept me up at night. It made me sad.

This sadness grew in September. The grapes failed to cheer me, though we harvested and boiled them in huge vats, more than we had ever boiled before.

The year seemed to be drawing to a good end. October was dry and November hardly rainy. The river did not roar, and its waters, remaining reasonable, did not invade our land, which was tilled in peace.

But all of my family's good fortune failed to ease my soul.

I was so melancholic that even the Christmas cold—that honest, sharp cold, which usually cheers me—failed to alter my mood. I spent a long, painful, gloomy winter.

I thought often of Gatzo. Where was he? Sometimes, at nightfall, high up in a cloud, ducks flew through a storm in a V. Their wild cries pierced me.

Seeing me so taciturn, my parents grew taciturn as well. They had tried everything, and nothing had worked. They remained worried.

Spring returned—warm winds, the bush warbler's first flight, the whistling blackbird. I sighed. And I hardly knew if it was from ease or from sorrow.

"Yes, he sighs," Tante Martine would say, "but perhaps it is a springtime sigh. I also sigh. And yet, as old as I am, it is still an April sigh."

To better watch over me, she had moved me to a room downstairs, right next to hers.

Sometimes, if I stirred on my soft cornhusk mattress behind the partition, she called me by name to see if I was awake or if I had had a bad dream. She was an astonishingly light sleeper. Because she was old and tired, I forced myself not to shift around in the bed when I was not asleep, so as not to wake her during the night. Then I would hear her breath moving through her like a thread of life.

She was asleep.

One night, I had a dream. Here is how it happened.

I had just dozed off. I was not quite awake, but I was not

fully asleep, at least not really. I am sure of it because my shutters had been left half-open, and through the cracks I could see two little stars sparkling. It seemed as if these shutters opened wider, bit by bit, and as they did, a vaster sky and a greater number of stars invaded my room. This invasion soon became so vast that the walls of the room disappeared and the open sky surrounded me. Little by little a strange landscape took shape, crystalline and studded with stars. It was the bottom of a luminous nighttime river, mysteriously lit from below by unseen fires. Their pale light flooded a secret, moving world of aquatic plants and animals; beneath this watery realm, where enormous trees plunged, I saw the roots of islands slowly breathing. Monsters with phosphorescent scales rose from the depths of hidden retreats, some of them bearing green and gold flares atop their spiny heads. Looking fierce, they calmly wandered through giant algae and meadows flowering with yarrow. Sometimes, a current drew along unbelievable creatures with milky bodies and changing shapes. They radiated a diffuse, quickly vanishing light. I saw living stars moving slowly on their five blue branches, while transparent conches and unknown shellfish swam through forests of fragile coral.

This world, revealed to me by the dream, troubled my sleep, and I sought in vain to leave these unreal places where everywhere malignant, watchful monsters were eyeing me. My desire must have been very strong (or I received some help from heaven) because little by little these illusory forms were erased from my dream, and instead of their inhuman and cruel beauty, I saw a familiar dawn, a morning sky, and a view of springtime in the countryside where my friend the river lazily flowed. And there I wandered gaily, through familiar places—the island of reeds, the cliff, the bank with the bubbling spring, the oak forest. Everything here enchanted me—birds, flowers, the free life, and especially a little rocky cove where, I recalled, I had often lingered to admire the limpid water during my days on the still waters.

It was a special spot. The crystalline rocks had created pure depths there, where the calm waves were cleansed.

Their transparence was so delicate the light circulated as easily as through the air, and the depths laughed with sunshine. On the yellow sand you could see blue porphyry and striated pink marble gravel. Under the rock, between the stones, an air bubble sometimes burst, evidence of a vein of water that secretly fed the limpid pool. It came from winter rains and snow-clad hills. It was what gave this little bit of river in this sheltered spot its unusual purity and the scent of living waters.

The water animals knew this place well, and I imagined it was a refuge for them, something like a liquid garden set aside for their games and play. They would not be devoured there, or that at least is what I thought.

Beneath a white water crowfoot lived a family of translucent little shrimp. Timid and active at the same time, they vanished at the slightest movement.

Every now and then, tempted by the water's coolness, a trout stopped by the pool, and silver bleaks on an outing lingered round, all atremble with delight. Less often, a speckled stickleback flashed its brilliant armature. If an iridescent gold tench, having wandered away from its hunting grounds, penetrated this clear wave, it snooped around, uncertain, and soon escaped for richer territories beyond this little mineral world. More familiar with these waters, a tree frog, a friend of pure depths, jumped in with its four feet spread wide, tumbling onto the fine sand; then it rose back up, wonderfully green. It set its delicate throat just above the water, and its golden eyes, mesmerizing my immobile face, were equally immobile with pleasure.

This double immobility, which I discovered in my dream, dissolved it. I fell sound asleep.

It was later in the night when someone scratched at the window and I awoke.

I was not afraid, but right away my heart started pounding.

"It is him," I thought. "He is back."

I leapt from my bed and ran to the window.

I called out. "Is it you, Gatzo?"

A voice murmured my name. It was a bit hoarse, but I recognized it.

"I have so much to tell you," Gatzo said.

In her room, Tante Martine sighed.

"Wait," I told Gatzo. "We better go down by the well."

I went outside.

We went to the well. It was nice down there.

The moon was rising peacefully at the far end of the warm, fragrant meadow.

And Gatzo began to talk.

He told me his whole story.

I listened in wonder. Suddenly he fell silent.

"And then?" I asked.

He answered me simply, "Grandfather Savinien died."

I took his hand.

At that moment, Tante Martine quietly opened her shutters. Did she see us?

She called to me. "Pascalet, my little one, with whom are you speaking?"

I rose mechanically and pulled Gatzo toward the house.

"Oh," cried Tante Martine, "is someone with you?"

"It is my friend Gatzo," I told her.

She took a noisy breath. "Oh, he smells wild."

I had the courage to add, "He is alone in the world, Tante Martine."

She muttered something.

Then she spoke. "Bring him in. Tomorrow we will brush him from head to toe."

Gatzo came in.

Tante Martine lit her candle.

"He is a solid little boy," she said when she saw Gatzo. "He looks honest. We will speak to your father about him."

What she said, no one will ever know. My father relented. God accomplished the rest.

And that is how Gatzo became my brother.

As for his story, perhaps I will tell it to you one day…

OTHER NEW YORK REVIEW CLASSICS

For a complete list of titles, visit www.nyrb.com.